U is for Utopia

An ABC Book about the Texas Hill Country

Written by Diane Causey
Illustrated by Bertie Salazar
Photo taken by Hattie Barham

"Dedicated to

Jordan, Aaron and Carson -

my partners in adventure throughout the

Texas Hill Country"

U is for *Utopia*

Texas Hill Country ABCs

Written by Diane Causey
Illustrated by Bertie Salazar

ISBN: 978-1-4269-8892-9

Trafford rev. 08/09/2011

Library of Congress Control Number: 2011913722

 www.trafford.com

North America & international
toll-free: 1 888 232 4444 (USA & Canada)
phone: 250 383 6864 ♦ fax: 812 355 4082

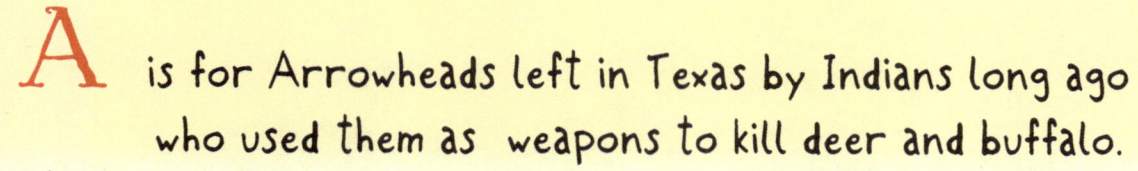

A is for Arrowheads left in Texas by Indians long ago who used them as weapons to kill deer and buffalo.

B is for the Big Dipper shining in the northern sky so bright.
This constellation gave pioneers a guiding light

4

C is for Campfire, feeling hot and smelling smokey,
where weiners are roasted and marshmellows are toasty.

D is for Deer roaming near and far,
in the fields, on the hills and in front of your car!

E is for Equine, a fancy name for a horse that can walk, trot or run.
At any gait you choose riding an equine can be fun.

F is for Floating the Frio River in a tube going fast or slow.
Slather on sunscreen, grab a hat and watch for big rocks below.

G is for Garner State Park where camps are lit by firefly flashes and rope swingers fill the river with great big splashes.

H is for Hummingbirds, tiny fighter pilots dive-bombing above your head
They like all colors but their favorite one is red.

I is for Indigo Snake, a special friend to man.
He slithers through the grass catching a rattler when he can.

J is for Jack Rabbit with ears long and tall. He likes to hop about but to see him scamper just give a loud shout.

K is for kids who come every summer from cities near and far to camps like LaJita, Lone Hollow, Mystic and Waldemar.

L is for Lost Maples Park where trees turn yellow, orange and red.
Find a straight stick to help you hike the winding, steep trails ahead.

M is for Mountains, though some prefer hills for a name,
It's these pretty humps that give Texas Hill Country it's fame.

N is for Nueces, a clear, beautiful river running so free.
The Spaniards named it for the nut of the native pecan tree.

O is for Ornery, a very stubborn and contrary way to act.
Donkeys, goats and even kids are sometimes ornery and that's a fact.

P is for Parade, Independence Day is the reason,
fireworks light up the sky at night to celebrate the season

Q is for Quarterback who leads his team on Friday night
Eagles, Owls, Panthers, Bobcats   FIGHT! FIGHT! FIGHT!

R is for Rodeo where pretty cowgirls carry our nation's flag so proud and cowboys try to ride bulls eight long seconds before a cheering crowd.

S is for Skipping rocks across the water so still
Throw a round, flat one and count the bounces for a thrill.

T is for Two-Stepping to the music of a good country song. Grab a partner, young or old, and dance right along.

U is for Utopia, a pretty little town where people are very nice
In fact, this town's name actually means Paradise.

V is for Verde Creek, the site of a camp in the days of the Calvary. Strange as it may be, these soldiers rode camels, not horses you see.

W is for Wildflowers blooming across the valleys, hills and roadways fine Bluebonnets, Pinks, Wine Cups, Daisies and even Green Milkweed Vine.

X is for XXOO which means hugs and kisses to you from me.
Put it on a postcard to Grandma and make her happy as can be.

Y is for Y'all, a word that means "you all" in Texas drawl.
Smile real big when you enter a room and say, "Howdy Y'all!"

Z is for Zero, the number of places you can travel to see that would be more beautiful than the Texas Hill Country.

www.ingramcontent.com/pod-product-compliance
Lightning Source LLC
Chambersburg PA
CBHW041543240626
47164CB00002B/113